This book belongs to

....

Quarto is the authority on a wide range of topics.
Quarto educates, entertains and enriches the lives of our readers—enthusiasts and lovers of hands-on living.
www.quartoknows.com

First published in 2019 by QED Publishing,
an imprint of The Quarto Group.
The Old Brewery, 6 Blundell Street,
London N7 9BH, United Kingdom.
T (0)20 7700 6700 F (0)20 7700 8066
www.QuartoKnows.com

A catalogue record for this book is available from the British Library.

ISBN 978-1-78603-598-1

Based on the original story by Steve Smallman

Author of adapted text: Katie Woolley
Series Editor: Joyce Bentley
Series Designer: Sarah Peden

Manufactured in Dongguan, China TL112018

9 8 7 6 5 4 3 2 1

Reading Gems

I Want to Be a Bat!

Bat flew into the sky.

Mouse made some bat wings.

I made some wings. I can fly!

Mouse tried again and again
but he could not fly.

Mouse fell with a bump!

Mum, I want to be a bat.

Mouse tried to sleep upside down.

Mouse could not sleep upside down.

Mouse tried to fly with his bat wings again.

He fell with a bump.

Mouse went
in a cave.

Bat was upside down
in the cave.

Bat flew down to Mouse
with a moth to eat.

Not a moth to eat!

I am a mouse.
I am not a bat!

Bat took Mouse into the sky.

Bat took Mouse to his mum.

Mum,
I can fly!

Story Words

Bat

bump

cave

flew

moth

mouse

Mum

sky

sleep

upside down

wings

Let's Talk About I Want to Be a Bat!

Look at the book cover.

Who is on the front of the book?

What is the animal doing?

Can you describe the setting?

In the story, Mouse wants to fly like Bat.

How does Mouse try to fly? What does he make?

Is Mouse able to fly? Why or why not?

Bat is asleep in the cave.

What is different about Bat's home and food?

What do you think Mouse would like to eat rather than a moth?

How does Mouse fly home?

What has Mouse learned while trying to be a bat?

Have you ever wanted to be something else?

Did you like the story?

What was the best bit?

Fun and Games

Look at the pictures and read the animal names underneath. Which name does not begin with the letter 'm'?

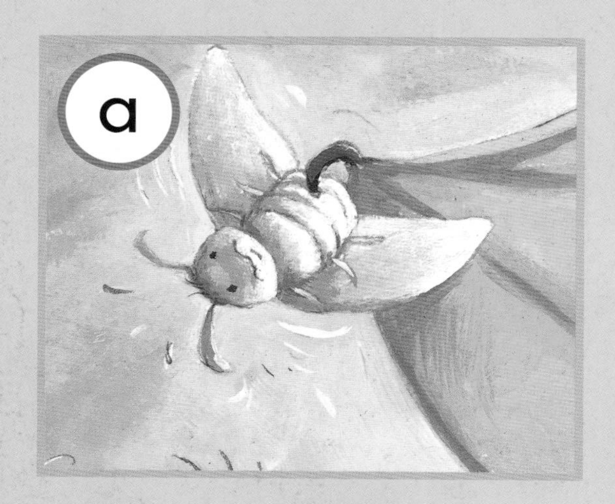

moth

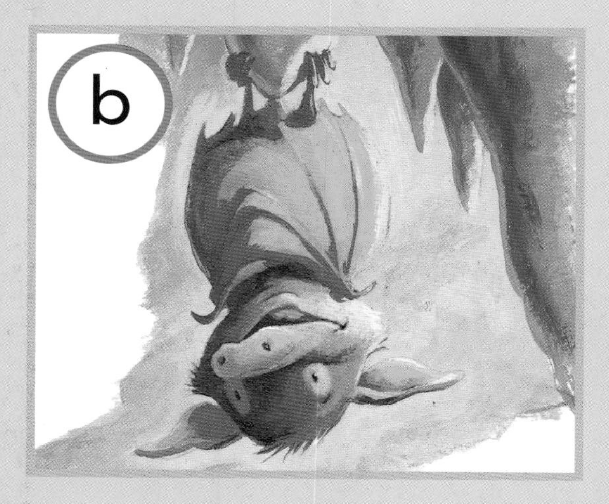

bat

mole

mouse

Answer: b: bat.

Sound out the words.
Then match them to the pictures.

moth

upside down

bump

fly

Answers: a: fly; b: bump; c: upside down; d: moth.

Your Turn

Now that you have read the story,
have a go at telling it in your own words.
Use the pictures below to help you.

5

6

7

8

GET TO KNOW READING GEMS

Reading Gems is a series of books that has been written for children who are learning to read. The books have been created in consultation with a literacy specialist.

The books fit into five levels, with each level getting more challenging as a child's confidence and reading ability grows. The simple text and fun illustrations provide gradual, structured practice of reading. Most importantly, these books are good stories that are fun to read!

Phonics is for children who are learning their letters and sounds. Simple, engaging stories provide gentle phonics practice.

Level 1 is for children who are taking their first steps into reading. Story themes and subjects are familiar to young children, and there is lots of repetition to build reading confidence.

Level 2 is for children who have taken their first reading steps and are becoming readers. Story themes are still familiar but sentences are a bit longer, as children begin to tackle more challenging vocabulary.

Level 3 is for children who are developing as readers. Stories and subjects are varied, and more descriptive words are introduced.

Level 4 is for readers who are rapidly growing in reading confidence and independence. There is less repetition on the page, broader themes are explored and plot lines straddle multiple pages.

I Want to Be a Bat! is all about a mouse who wants to fly. It explores themes of personal identity, differences and friendship.